HORSE DIARIES
· Bell's Star ·

HORSE DIARIES

HORSE DIARIES

Bell's Star

ALISON HART

illustrated by RUTH SANDERSON

RANDOM HOUSE NEW YORK

Text copyright © 2009 by Alison Hart
Illustrations copyright © 2009 by Ruth Sanderson
Photograph on p. 110 © Juniors Bildarchiv/Alamy

Published in the United States by Random House Children's Books,
a division of Random House, Inc., New York.

Random House and the colophon are registered trademarks of Random House, Inc.

Visit us on the Web! www.randomhouse.com/kids

Educators and librarians, for a variety of teaching tools, visit us at
www.randomhouse.com/teachers

Library of Congress Cataloging-in-Publication Data
Hart, Alison.
Bell's Star / by Alison Hart ; illustrated by Ruth Sanderson. — 1st ed.
p.   cm. — (Horse diaries ; #2)
Summary: In the Vermont spring of 1853, Bell's Star, a Morgan horse, and his owner Katie rescue a runaway slave and try to outwit the slave catchers in order to help her to freedom.
ISBN 978-0-375-85204-6 (trade) — ISBN 978-0-375-95204-3 (lib. bdg.)
1. Morgan horse—Juvenile fiction. [1. Morgan horse—Fiction. 2. Horses—Fiction. 3. Fugitive slaves—Fiction. 4. Slavery—Fiction. 5. Vermont—History—19th century—Fiction.] I. Sanderson, Ruth, ill. II. Title.
PZ10.3.H247Be 2009   [Fic]—dc22   2007049698

Printed in the United States of America

30 29 28

First Edition

To all who have found freedom.

—A.H.

For my lovely models, Naomi and Imani,
and special thanks to Courtney and Jessie and
their beautiful Morgans.

—R.S.

CONTENTS

"Oh! if people knew what a comfort to horses a light hand is . . ."
—from *Black Beauty*, by Anna Sewell

HORSE DIARIES

· Bell's Star ·

1

Vermont, Early Spring 1850

I was born in a rocky paddock on a cloudy night. Light snow fell from the sky, covering my brown fur with white. My mother's tongue washed over me and warmed my skin. Soon she nudged me, urging me to stand.

Rise, she told me. *Danger can hide in the dark woods.*

I scrambled to my feet. My long legs were sturdy, my body stout. I nursed, and my mother's milk gave me strength. I hopped in the snow, trying out my legs. Mother smiled proudly as I trotted and leaped. Soon I grew weary. Mother led me into the shed, and sinking onto a soft pile of hay, I slept.

Morning came, and the rising sun broke through the clouds. As soon as it was light, my mother began to teach me.

There is so much to learn, she told me. I followed her around the paddock. She touched her nose to all the new things: *fence, tree, water trough, hay, mud.*

Mud I learned quickly. As the snow

melted, my tiny hooves sank into the sloppy brown mess. I was scrambling onto a dry stump when a fluttering sound startled me.

A bright blue creature landed on the fence. I tensed. *Is this danger?* I asked my mother.

Her muzzle twitched in laughter. *No, my son. That is a blue jay. They are pesky and steal my corn, but they are not danger.*

Jumping off the stump, I whinnied to the blue jay. It flew into the trees.

Blue jays have wings, my mother explained. *They are free to fly to wherever they want.*

I peered between the fence rails. I wanted to race after the blue jay to the place called *wherever they want*. The blue jay had disappeared, but outside the paddock were many more new things to explore!

I touched my nose to the railing, but the fence circled my mother and me, penning us in. I checked my back. Did I have wings? All I saw was brown hair.

If only I had wings, I thought. *I could fly free, too.*

Suddenly a shriek filled the air. I fled behind my mother. I flicked my fuzzy ears. *Danger?* Turning, I peeked from beneath her thick black tail.

A creature leaped over the top railing, landing with a splash in the mud. It was as colorful and noisy as the blue jay, only bigger! Wings spread wide, it hurtled toward me.

Terrified, I turned to run, but my long legs tangled. I fell in a heap. Mud splattered my white star. The giant blue jay plopped on the ground next to me. Its wings wrapped tightly around my neck, and I was trapped!

Mother, I neighed. *Danger!*

But my mother's eyes were twinkling.

"Papa! Bell had her foal!" the blue jay cried out.

"I see, Miss Katie," an even taller blue jay answered. "But, daughter, your joy is scaring him. Let him go so we can see how fine he is."

The wings released me. I scrambled to my hooves and rushed to the far side of the paddock. My mother hurried after me and blew into my nostrils.

Do not be afraid. Those are humans. The large one is Papa. The small one is Katie. They feed and care for us. In return, we work for them.

Work. I did not know that word yet.

My mother pushed me forward. My legs splayed, refusing to move. The human called Papa set a wooden bucket in the paddock. "Come, Bell," he called. My mother trotted over. Dipping her head, she ate hungrily.

"You have given us a fine fellow, Bell," Papa said, patting her neck.

Wide-eyed and trembling, I stared at the human called Katie. She stood in the middle of the paddock, her eyes as curious as mine. Then she held out one wing.

This time she walked quietly to me. Her wings were soft when they stole around my

neck. Then her cheek pressed against mine,
and my trembling stopped.

"He has a white star, just like Bell," Katie
said. "And look, two white legs."

"He's a fine-looking Morgan horse. Strong like his dam. Handsome like his sire," Papa said. "Soon he'll be able to pull the plow and the carriage."

"Papa, may I name him?" Katie asked.

He nodded.

"I name him Bell's Star."

"That's a grand name for such a small foal," Papa said.

"One day he *will* be grand, I know," Katie said, scratching my fuzzy mane. "He'll lead the St. Albans parade like Mr. Jones's Morgan horse."

"Let's hope he grows up to be as grand a worker as Bell," Papa said. "Our farm needs a Morgan that can pull a plow, not lead a parade."

I nuzzled Katie's arm. I didn't know *grand* or *parade*, but I wanted to show her I no longer thought she was *danger*.

"Oh, Papa," Katie sighed, her breath tickling my whiskers. "I love him already."

"We'll give Bell a day of rest," Papa said. "Then it's back to work tomorrow."

Work. There was that word again. That morning, with Katie's arms around my neck, I thought nothing more of it.

But soon I would know what it meant.

2

Vermont, Early Spring 1853

Tail held high, I trotted uphill through
woods. My hooves dug into the thawing
ground. Behind me, the wagon bed rattled.
All around me, maple trees rose into the sky,
their bare branches casting shadows across
the melting snow.

I shook my head, and the bit jingled in my mouth. The harness straps snapped my back, and the traces jostled my sides.

"Whoa, Star," Katie called from the wagon seat. I halted before a thick grove of maple trees. Buckets filled with maple sap hung from spouts in the tree trunks. Katie jumped from the wagon.

I turned my head to watch Katie lift a heavy bucket off the spout. She dragged it over. Grunting, she lifted the bucket onto the wagon bed. Then she climbed into the bed and poured the maple sap into one of the barrels.

The afternoon was warm, and sweat stained my brown neck. Sweat dripped down Katie's brow as she hooked the bucket

back onto the spout and then hurried along
to the next tree.

This, I had learned, was work.

For the first year of my life, I frolicked by my mother's side while she worked. The human called Papa rose at dawn. He harnessed Bell and they worked until dusk. Plowing and planting, mowing and sowing, pulling and dragging. Farm chores were never ending. Papa was lucky, though, because not all farmers had a strong Morgan to help them.

When I was two, I began doing light work. I pulled the human called Mama to town in the carriage. I carried Katie to school. She'd leap on my back and we'd canter wildly through the snow to the schoolhouse. Katie pretended she was a princess or an explorer. I pretended I could fly to *wherever I wanted*.

But now I was three and my mother was growing tired. Now Bell pulled Mama in the carriage and carried Katie to school. I took over Bell's jobs. From dawn until dusk, I worked with Papa. When the days grew longer and warmer, Katie came home early from school. Often she worked alongside me. Those were the times I loved best.

"This is the last maple grove," Katie said as she dumped another bucket. "If we beat Papa home, we'll have time for a gallop. How's that sound, Star?"

I pricked my ears at the word *gallop*. I missed carrying Katie to school. I missed pretending I could race to *wherever I wanted*.

Katie dumped the last bucket. "Done!"

She walked around the wagon to my head. She scratched under my long forelock, and my lips wiggled in delight.

She laughed. "I'm glad *you're* happy. Mama may give me a whipping when she sees my pinafore." It was splattered with mud, as were my stockings.

"But if Mama does have a fit, I'll say to her, tell Papa *no more work*. Then I can go to school all day and you can eat sweet spring grass, and neither of us will be dirty."

My stomach rumbled. I snatched at a bush, but the dead leaves tasted bitter. Katie dug in the pocket of her pinafore. She held out a dried apple. "Don't tell Bell. She'll want one, too, but it's the last in the barrel. Winter has been too long."

The reins flapped against my neck as I chewed.

"Come on. Let's take these barrels to the sugar shack. Mama needs to get the sap boiling." With one last pat, Katie climbed onto the wagon seat.

As soon as Katie sat down, I set off at a brisk trot. She didn't need to slap the reins. I knew from her tone she was eager to get back, and I was eager to be free of the harness.

We trotted for a mile, but the lane grew muddier. The wheels sank. The wagon stopped.

"Oh no." Katie groaned as she looked over the side. All four wheels were stuck. "If we don't hurry, we won't have time for a ride to the river."

I knew *river*. The water would wash the

mud off my stockings and the sweat off my neck.

Digging my hooves into the mud, I strained against the harness. The wagon rocked forward, and the front wheels popped free.

"Go, Star, go!" Katie urged.

Like all Morgan horses, I was strong for my size. Last fall, I had dragged a huge tree from the forest. Compared to that, Katie and the barrels weighed little. Taking a deep breath, I pulled harder. The back wheels jerked free, and we were on our way!

Shaking my long, thick mane, I broke into a trot. Katie sang with delight as she bounced on the wooden seat. The barrels rattled as I pulled the wagon into the farm-yard, scattering the chickens.

I stopped in front of the small barn. Papa had built it last fall using boards cut from the huge tree. Katie unhooked the traces, and I stepped from between the wagon shafts. She unbuckled the harness and the bridle. As the last strap fell free, I shook happily.

"We've got to hurry. Papa will be here any minute." Katie slipped the halter onto my head and hooked ropes to the rings. "It's not yet sundown, so he's sure to want me to fetch water or feed the chickens."

I stood beside a stump so she could mount. Tucking her skirt around her legs, she leaped onto my back. Her fingers twined in my mane. I trotted off before her legs touched my sides.

To the river!

"Katie! We need to unload the sap!" Mama hollered. She stood in front of the sugar shack, which was built beside the barn.

I heard her calling, but Katie's heels nudged me into a canter.

And we were gone.

The River

I cantered down the farm's lane. Turning sharply, I raced through the hay field. As with all Morgans, my gait was smooth. My legs rose with a fancy *snap*.

Katie whooped. We were free!

The field sloped to the river, which

wound like a snake at the bottom of the hill. The sun was beginning to sink, casting a glow on the water.

Katie clung tightly to my mane as I trotted downhill. Brush grew thick along the river, and briars and twigs snagged my legs. The bank was steep, and I trod carefully to the river's edge.

I waded into the chilly water. Dipping my head, I drank. With a happy sigh, Katie lay upon my mane. Her arms dangled on both sides of my neck.

Except for my slurping and the water's gurgling, all was quiet.

Then I heard a sound. A *gasp*. It was the same gasp that Mama made when she discovered a fox had killed her chickens.

The same gasp Papa made when Katie tumbled from the new barn roof.

Like a horse's snort, it was the sound of fear.

And the sound hadn't come from Katie.

I raised my head. Water dripped from my mouth. Ahead of me was a tangle of branches in deeper water. A human clung to one of the branches. It was a girl human, like Katie. Except this girl's skin was as brown as my own coat.

The girl gasped again. Her eyes were white, like a horse's eyes when it senses danger.

The branches she clung to were beginning to shift. I flicked my ears, understanding the trouble. The current was about to sweep the branches and the girl downriver.

I gave a low whinny, alerting Katie. She
popped upright on my back. "What is it,
Star?" she asked.

I sloshed into the swirling water until it was chest-deep. Katie's legs hugged my sides. Did she see the girl, too? There was no time to find out.

The rushing water dislodged the branches a little more. They spun, and water lapped at the girl's head. Quickly, I reached her. Her eyes met mine and then flicked upward to Katie, who yelled to her, "Take my hand!"

Hurry, I whinnied.

Katie bent lower, her arm outstretched. The branches broke free just as the girl let go. With one hand, she grasped Katie's hand. With the other, she caught my mane. The water tugged at her, trying to carry her downstream, but she wound her fingers in the long strands of my mane.

I swung left, yanking my right hoof from the mud. The girl's weight pulled me off balance, and I fell to my knees. I raised my nose high, but she went under.

Reaching down, Katie grabbed the girl's elbow and pulled her to the surface. I found my balance and rose up. With a mighty effort, I lunged for the bank. The girl coughed and sputtered, but she didn't let go. Katie held tightly to her elbow, and together we dragged her toward shore.

The water was now knee-deep. My hooves found hard bottom and I scrambled onto the bank.

The girl let go of my mane and plopped onto a rock. Katie slid off my back. My sides heaved as I caught my breath.

"You were wonderful, Star," Katie said, hugging my soaked neck.

Tilting my head, I stared down at the girl. Katie stared at her, too. Her mane was as black as mine, but shorter and braided. Her wet dress was like Katie's—sprinkled with flowers—but hers was as worn as an old feed sack.

Raising her head, the girl stared at us. Her eyes were tired, but thankful, too.

I blew softly on her cheek, and she stroked my muzzle. Then she lowered her gaze. "Thank you, kind mistress," she whispered. "You and your horse saved me."

She scrambled to her bare feet. Her arms hugged the front of her wet dress, and she trembled with the cold. "I best be on my way."

"On your way?" Katie said. "But you're cold and wet."

"Yes, mistress," the girl said, "but I still have to go."

"Where are you going? Why were you in the river?" Katie asked.

"I cannot say." Eyes downcast, the girl turned as if to run, but she swayed dizzily.

Katie caught her arm to hold her up. "Perhaps you should rest first."

"No, mistress," the girl said. "My mama waits for me."

"Where is she waiting? Star and I could take you to her," Katie said.

"Oh no! I cannot tell, cannot—" The girl glanced up the riverbank. Again I saw fear in her eyes, as if *danger* hid in the hay field.

"You're a runaway slave, aren't you?" Katie asked softly.

The girl yanked her arm from Katie's grasp. "No!"

"Don't be afraid," said Katie. "Star and I can help you find your mama. But you're tired and wet. You need to rest until morning."

"No, I must go." The girl took one step, but her legs buckled and she sank to the rock.

Katie kneeled next to her. "You need a blanket and food. Come. You can hide in our barn tonight."

The girl shook her head. "Canada is so close. I must get there tonight!"

"Canada is miles away. It will be dark. Come with us to the barn. Star will watch over you," Katie said. "You can leave for Canada tomorrow. Then you will be dry and well fed."

Lowering my head, I nuzzled the girl's cheek. Her skin was icy, and I could feel her shiver.

"Will you trust us?" Katie asked gently.

Reaching up, the girl cupped my muzzle with her trembling fingers, and then she nodded. "Yes."

The Runaway

"Good." Katie jumped to her feet. "Now we have to hurry or Papa will worry."

"You cannot tell him!" the girl exclaimed.

"I will not. I promise. But if Star and I don't get home, he'll come searching for us."

Katie helped the girl to her feet. "My name's Katie."

"I'm . . . I'm Eliza," the girl said.

"Pleased to meet you, Eliza," Katie said. "You can ride Star."

Eliza looked at me with big eyes. "I've never been on a horse."

"It's not hard," Katie said. "And you're too weary to walk."

Katie boosted her up. "Hold on to his mane. He's a Morgan horse, so his back is broad and comfortable. And he'll warm you."

Katie led the way up the bank and through the brush. I walked carefully so as not to unseat Eliza. She was as light as a crow, so I barely felt her weight.

"Why are you running to Canada?" Katie

asked as we walked through the hay field. "How did you get swept into the river? How were you parted from your mama?"

Eliza didn't reply. Her fingers dug into my withers as she slipped from side to side. Finally Katie stopped her chattering. We walked in silence down the lane. When we were almost to the barn, Katie halted. She put a finger to her lips. By then dusk was upon us, and the farmyard was filled with shadows. Earlier, Eliza had stopped trembling, but now I felt her shake again. Was our farmyard *danger*?

Katie ran ahead and into the barn. When she waved, I trotted through the wide doorway.

I halted, and Eliza slipped off. Quickly,

Katie led her behind the hay mound, which was low because of the long winter.

From the corner of the barn, Patsy the milk cow watched us. Bell stared at us from her stall. I wanted to tell my mother what was going on. I wanted to ask her if she knew the words *runaway*, *slave*, and *Canada*. But I heard Papa's boot steps outside the barn.

"Katie!"

Katie shot from behind the hay mound, scaring the chickens scratching in the dirt. I trotted into my stall. Grabbing a brush, she hurried in after me just as Papa marched into the barn. His face was red, so I knew he was angry.

"Where have you been?" Papa asked. "It is past supper. Your mother has been worried."

"We were at the river," Katie explained. "Star and I were so hot and muddy. We wanted to wash off."

Papa looked over the stall door, his dark brows raised. Katie's pinafore was as speckled as a white and brown hen. I was muddy from my stockings to my chest.

He frowned at her. "The truth, my daughter?"

"We fell in the river," she said sheepishly. "I'm sorry, sir."

Papa sighed. "Groom Star carefully. Feed him extra corn. Tomorrow he has to plow."

Corn I knew, and my mouth watered excitedly. *Plow* I also knew from my mother's work last year. That did not excite me.

Papa pointed a finger at Katie. "And you will help, too."

"But I'll miss school," Katie said.

"That is your punishment for leaving your mama. She had to unload the sap alone while you frolicked in the river," he said.

Katie hung her head. "Yes, sir."

"Mama left supper on the table," Papa said. "So be quick about your chores."

As soon as Papa left, Katie fed me a bucket of corn. Then she shook out Bell's old saddle blanket and took it to Eliza.

When Katie was finished, she kissed my nose. "I'll return when it's safe. I promised Eliza I'd help her find her mother. Will you help me keep that promise?"

I chewed my corn, not sure what my

mistress was asking. When Katie left, I joined Bell at the back of the stalls. We could see Eliza, who was curled up in the hay. The blanket was wrapped around her and she was fast asleep. *Who is this strange human?* my mother asked.

I told her all that had happened, puffing my chest a bit when I spoke of the rescue. Then I asked, *What are* runaways, slaves, *and* Canada?

I only know what I hear when I go to school with Katie, she said. *Katie's teacher says slaves are humans who are not free. They can't go to school. They work all day. Sometimes they're whipped. Runaways are humans who want to be free. Some run north to Canada. There they can be free.*

Thinking about my mother's words, I went back to my feed bucket and licked up the last kernel. I knew about *north*, *work*, and wanting to be free. And I had seen Mr. Jenkins whip his mule, Tansy. The crack of the whip made me shudder even now.

I understood why Eliza had run away and why she wanted to be free. But I had never heard of Canada. Was it so different from our farm? And if I went north, I wondered, would I be free, too?

5

The Sheriff

The next day, before it was daylight, Katie crept into the barn. She had a basket in her arms.

Patsy mooed for her morning hay. I started to whinny for my corn. But Katie put a finger to her lips. Without even glancing at the corn bin, she disappeared behind the hay mound.

Eliza had been so quiet all night, I'd forgotten about her. Now I turned in my stall to see behind the mound. The two girls sat in the hay, sharing food from the basket. One of Katie's shawls was around Eliza's shoulders.

Bell stirred in her stall. She'd been lying down, sleeping. Now she stood and shook. *Why is Katie here so early?* she asked.

Not to feed us, I grumbled. I kicked the wall, reminding Katie she should share some hay with Patsy, my mother, and *me*.

Katie jumped up. "Don't be so impatient, Star." Picking up the pitchfork, she tossed a forkful of hay to each of us. Then she went back to Eliza.

"As soon as it's light enough to see, we'll leave," Katie said. "You can ride Bell. She's gentle. I'll lead you across the river to the road north. Perhaps your mama will be waiting."

Eliza nodded as she hungrily ate a biscuit. Then she swallowed. "Won't your papa be angry if you leave?" she asked.

"I'll tell him that Star ran away and I had to ride Bell to catch him."

I popped my head up. Hay dangled from my mouth. *Run away?* That sounded fun.

"You would do that for me?" Eliza asked.

"Yes." Katie nodded. "It's a lie, I know. And if Papa finds out, I'll have to help plow for a fortnight. But you need to be with your mama. You need to be free."

Standing, Katie picked up the basket. "And I need to tack up the horses. Come. You can meet Bell."

Katie took my bridle off the wooden peg. When she opened my stall door, I put my head in the corner. I did not want to be bridled so early. I wanted to finish my hay!

But then I remembered how Tansy had been cut with the whip, and I did not want Eliza whipped, too.

Katie put the metal bit in my mouth and slipped the headstall over my ears. Then she gave me a big hug. "Thank you for helping, Star."

Eliza was in Bell's stall. She was timidly patting her neck. My mother snuffled her gently, telling her not to be afraid.

Katie opened my stall and led me to the barn door. The sky was turning light, but fog had settled in during the night. I saw the glow of a candle in the window of the house and heard someone cough from inside.

"Papa's awake," Katie whispered. "We have to leave now."

Katie dropped my reins to help Eliza with Bell. I pricked my ears, suddenly hearing the *thud, thud* of a horse's hooves. Someone was coming up the lane!

Was it *danger*? I pawed the ground, trying to warn Katie. "Be still, Star," Katie called from inside the barn.

Tossing my head, I peered out the barn door. The air was thick with fog, but I could smell a horse. It was Dover, the horse belonging to the human called the sheriff. *Why is the sheriff here so early?* I wondered. I whinnied to Dover, and he whinnied back, alerting Katie that someone was coming.

"Hide, Eliza!" Katie cried out.

I heard the scampering of feet behind me and the slam of Bell's stall. Then the front door of the house opened, and Papa came onto the step. Holding up the lamp, he tried to see through the morning mist.

"Katie? Are you in the barn?" he called.

"Yes, Papa." Katie hurried to stand beside me. "I was feeding Star. I knew you wanted to start plowing early."

Just then Dover and the sheriff appeared through the fog.

"Morning, Miss Katie," the sheriff greeted her. "Morning, Hiram," he called to Papa on the step.

"Morning," Papa called. "What brings you to our farm this morning? I hope it isn't bad news."

"Not bad news, Hiram." The sheriff dismounted.

Dover snorted, and I snorted back. Dover was a strong Morgan horse, too. He carried the sheriff from farm to farm. I tugged on the reins in Katie's hand. Horses are herd animals, so we love to meet others of our kind.

Katie led me toward Dover and we touched noses. Dover and I squealed and Katie scolded us. "Hush," she whispered. "I want to hear what the sheriff tells Papa."

"I'm riding to all the farms along the river," the sheriff said. "I received a telegraph yesterday concerning runaway slaves, a mother and daughter, traveling through Vermont into Canada."

I felt Katie tense beside me. Hooking her fingers into my mane, she held on tightly.

"The mother and daughter were seen crossing the river below town," the sheriff continued. "A witness said the daughter was swept downstream."

"I've seen no runaways," Papa said. "And like most Vermonters, I don't agree with slavery. Let them run to freedom, I say. All people should be free."

The sheriff nodded. "I know how folks in this area feel about slavery," he said. "But the new law says we have to help return them to Southern owners." He pulled out a paper from his saddlebag. "The telegraph states there's a reward. One hundred dollars for any information leading to the capture of the runaway slaves Honesty and Eliza."

Runaways. Eliza. I knew those words. But I had never heard of *law* or *reward*.

"A hundred dollars is a mighty sum," Papa said. "The winter was hard. That reward would buy seed and pay debts."

Katie gasped. "Papa! You wouldn't trade a person for seed!"

"Hush, daughter. This is a matter for grown-ups," Papa said. "Not that the reward concerns us. We have no knowledge of the runaways."

"Let me know if you hear or see something," the sheriff said. "It's better that folks in Vermont catch the mother and daughter. At least we'll treat them with kindness." He held up the telegraph. "The Southern owner has sent slave catchers after the runaways.

They're arriving by railroad this morning."
The sheriff frowned at Katie. "Slave catchers
aren't like us, Miss Katie. No telling what
they'll do if they catch those two."

Katie turned white. I nudged her shoulder, thinking about Eliza hiding behind the
hay mound. *If Papa knew she was in the barn,
would he turn her in?* I wondered. And even
worse, *Who are these humans called slave
catchers, and what will they do if they catch
Eliza?*

6

Slave Catchers!

Tipping his hat, the sheriff said, "Thank you for your time, Hiram. Send word if you see those runaways."

Papa nodded. "I'd like to be of help, but as I said, there has been no sign."

The sheriff mounted Dover. "I'm off to

see Miss Biddle. Rumor around town says she's one of the folks who help runaways escape."

"Miss Biddle? My teacher?" Katie asked.

I knew the human Miss Biddle. She fed me dried apples when I went to school.

"Yes, miss," the sheriff replied. "Rumor has it she's helped more than a few slaves find their way to Canada. Now I best be on my way," he said. He reined Dover around, and they trotted off.

Papa waved farewell and then shook his head. "Miss Biddle is foolish."

I could feel Katie's arm shaking against me. Was she afraid for Eliza? But then she stamped her foot like an angry horse.

"Miss Biddle is not foolish," Katie

declared. "She's right. Slaves are people, too. They should be free. Please don't help the sheriff, Papa."

Papa shook his head. "You are too young to understand, daughter." He blew out the flame in the lantern. Setting it on the step, he headed to the barn. I whinnied to Bell, letting her know that Papa was coming. Would she warn Eliza?

Patsy mooed hungrily. Katie and I trotted into the barn after Papa. Dropping my reins, Katie quickly ran to the hay mound to give Patsy another forkful of hay. "There, Papa. Patsy is fed."

"Thank you, Katie. You are being very helpful this morning." While Patsy chewed, he pulled the stool over to milk her. "So, daughter, why is Star bridled?" he asked as the milk squirted into the bucket.

Katie flushed red. *Does Papa know our secret?* I wondered.

I glanced uneasily at the hay mound. There was no sign of Eliza, and Bell was calmly eating the last stalks of her hay.

"Umm, well, I hoped to ride Star before plowing," Katie said.

"You mean you hoped to race him wildly through the fields," Papa said.

"Yes, sir."

He sighed. "Daughter, life is hard work. Don't you think I'd rather race than plow? Farmer Harvey boasts that his Thoroughbred,

Liberty, can beat any Morgan horse in the county. Don't you think I'd like to prove him wrong?"

I tossed my head excitedly. Racing! Why, Katie and I had already beaten Billy

Barton and his Thoroughbred, Prince. Like many Morgans, I'm only fifteen hands high, but I'm as fast as lightning.

Katie perked up. "Oh, can we, Papa? Star can beat that old Liberty any day!"

Papa sighed again. "No, Katie. What if Star got a stone bruise or broke his wind? How would we plant spring crops? How would we clear the new potato field?"

"I understand, Papa," she said.

"Harness Star. Then run into the house. Mama's putting noon meal in a basket. We'll be in the fields all day."

All day! I knew what *all day* meant. It meant I would be stiff and sore when we trod home at dusk. It meant no splashing in the river or galloping *wherever we wanted*. And it meant that we wouldn't be able to help Eliza find her mother.

Katie's shoulders fell, so I could tell she knew what it meant, too. "Yes, sir." Katie walked over to the pegs. As she lifted the harness, she asked, "Papa, what are slave catchers?"

"They are men paid to hunt runaway slaves," he replied. "When they catch the slaves, they take them south to their owners."

"What if they don't want to go back? What if they want to be free?" she asked.

"Slaves belong to their owners," Papa said. "That is the way in the South. They cannot choose to be slave or free."

"That is wrong," Katie said. "And if I

met a slave, I would be like Miss Biddle and help her run to freedom."

Papa stood up so fast the stool fell over. "You would not!" He shouted so loudly that I startled and Katie dropped the harness. "The new law says that no one can help runaways." He pointed his finger at Katie. "And that includes fathers and their meddling daughters."

Picking up the milk bucket, he added sternly, "There will be no more talk about runaways. Finish your chores. We leave for the field in ten minutes."

As soon as Papa left, Katie scurried behind the hay mound. I could hear her whispering to Eliza. I heard *promise, tonight,* and *north*. Katie was as stubborn as Tansy the mule. I knew that despite Papa's harsh words, my mistress would soon be helping Eliza.

The warm sun shone upon my back. I plodded in a straight line, straining against the harness as the plow blade cut through the hard dirt. A pesky black fly settled on my rump, and I wiggled my skin and switched my tail.

Behind me, Papa guided the plow. I swerved to shake off the fly. "Gee," he called, telling me to move right. "Haw," when I went too far.

Behind Papa, Katie walked in the new furrows. Bending, she picked up stones and rocks. She carried the large stones to a pile for fencing. The small ones she tossed in a sack.

The three of us had been working all morning.

The fly bit me and I kicked out. Papa hollered at me to settle down. I snorted, tired of the stinging flies, the endless back and forth, the chafing harness, and the sun.

When will it be time to race to wherever I want? I wondered. And more importantly, *When will it be time to rest?*

Finally Papa said, "Noon meal, Katie." He unhitched the trace chains and steered me to the shade of a pine tree. The pungent smell of the needles helped keep the flies away. The shade cooled my back. A bucket of water waited for me; a basket waited for Papa and Katie.

Katie followed us, the sack of stones

banging against her skirt. Under her bonnet, her face was as sweaty as mine and a fly bite swelled on her cheek. She took the bit from my mouth so I could drink.

Papa opened the basket. He handed Katie a baked sweet potato, its skin orange and wrinkly. I eyed it with interest, and Katie fed me a morsel. It was cold and sweet.

"You best eat, daughter," Papa said.

"Star needs it more than I," Katie replied. "He's been plowing all morning."

"And you've been picking rocks all morning."

"You always say that a family needs to share the chores—and the food," Katie said stubbornly. "And Star is part of our family."

Family. I liked the sound of that word.

Papa frowned, so I thought he didn't like the word, but then he laughed. "Daughter, you and Tansy the mule must be cousins."

Holding out her palm, Katie fed me a corner of her hoecake. Just then I heard the sound of hoofbeats coming from the direction of the farm. Was my mother coming to visit?

Two strange horses cantered over the hill. Papa spotted them, too. He stood, shading his eyes.

"Who's that?" Katie asked as she jumped to her feet.

"I don't know," Papa said. "They're not neighbors or townsfolk."

Raising my head, I whinnied. The horses did not whinny back.

"Step behind Star, Katie," Papa said as

they cantered closer, and Katie hid herself by my off side.

Papa stood beside me and placed his hand on my neck. Two men rode tall in the

saddle. They held the reins tightly, and their horses tossed their heads as if the bits hurt their mouths.

The men pulled their horses sharply to a stop. The horses were as long-legged as Liberty the Thoroughbred. I saw marks on the sides of their bellies from their riders' sharp spurs. One of them held a whip.

"Good afternoon, gentlemen," Papa greeted them.

The taller man asked, "Are you Hiram Landry?"

"Yes, I am," Papa replied. "How can I help you?"

"We're hunting for two runaways seen crossing the river yesterday. A witness said one of them, a girl, was swept downstream."

Papa nodded. "So the sheriff told me this morning."

The taller man spat on the ground. "Your farm is downstream from there. We aim to hunt for her here."

I flicked my ears, hearing *mean* in the man's voice. The smaller man's horse pawed nervously, and his rider yanked the reins.

I felt Katie creep closer to my head. Turning, I blew softly on her shoulder. Flipping back her bonnet, she cupped her palms around my muzzle. "Those men must be the slave catchers who want Eliza," she whispered. "But, Star, we have promised to keep her safe. And we must keep our promise!"

Katie's Plan

"Who's that hiding behind the horse?" the tall man hollered. "Show yourself!"

I swung my head back around. The rider spurred his horse toward me, but I pinned my ears. Flipping his whip off the saddle horn, he uncoiled it. "Get your horse out of my way," he growled to Papa. "I aim to find out who you're hiding."

Papa stepped between us. "Coil your whip. It's my daughter," he said quickly, pulling Katie protectively against him.

The tall man scowled as he rolled up his whip.

The smaller man said, "If you help us, Mr. Landry, there's a mighty nice reward."

"I know of the reward," Papa replied. "But I know nothing about runaway slaves. Even if I did, I wouldn't give them up to you."

"Courageous words from a poor dirt farmer with a runt of a horse," the taller man scoffed.

I did not know *runt*, but from the tone of his voice, I knew it was not kind. I swished my tail. I did not like how these slave hunters talked and treated their horses.

"My Morgan's worth four of your horses," Papa said angrily. "Not only is he stronger, but he's faster."

The two men burst out laughing. "Faster than our Thoroughbreds? I doubt those boastful words."

"Now kindly ride off my *poor* farm," Papa said. "If you do not, I'll have the sheriff arrest you for trespassing."

The tall man pointed the handle of his whip at Papa. "We'll catch those slaves without your help," he declared. Reining their horses around, the two men cantered across our newly plowed field, leaving deep gashes in the dirt.

Papa's face reddened. Katie flung her arms around his waist. "You were so brave, Papa!" Then she hugged me, too. "Imagine calling you a runt, Star. Papa's right—you could beat their horses in a race any day!"

I stamped my feet, ready to gallop, but the trace chains banged against my sides. Looking at the hoofprints dug into the field, I knew there would be no racing today. Only more plowing.

"Gather the basket and bucket, Katie," Papa said. "We have work to finish."

"Yes, Papa." Katie fed me the last hoe-cake. As I munched, I thought about Eliza and the slave catchers and I knew Katie was right. We had to keep our promise.

That night, my legs ached from dragging the plow. My sides ached from straining against the harness. I chewed my hay slowly, almost too tired to eat.

It was late and the barn was dark. Katie

and Papa had long ago gone into the house. Bell was tuckered from pulling Mama and a load of syrup to town. Patsy was outside in the paddock, grazing. The chickens roosted on the lid of the corn bin.

My eyelids fluttered shut. I dreamed I was galloping through a meadow of flowers. Blue jays flew beside me, leading the way to *wherever I wanted*. Katie clung to my mane, laughing.

I heard rustling coming from outside, and my eyes popped open. A shape darted into the barn on silent feet. Fingers lightly touched my neck. "Star, it's me," Katie whispered. "I've come to keep my promise to Eliza."

Sleepily, I flapped my lips. Then I heard

Katie whispering to Eliza. I heard *slave catchers*, followed by a sharp cry from Eliza.

I shook, trying to wake up. Bell's head was hanging over her stall door. *What is happening?* she asked.

Tonight we take Eliza north to find her mother, I told her.

With no light to guide her, Katie bridled us both. When she led me to the barn door, I could see that daylight was far away. I peered past the farmyard to the forest. The trees rose black and thick into the sky. *Will danger find us tonight?* I wondered.

I stared at the forest, listening for strange sounds. I heard the *whoo* of an owl and the jingle of a horse's bit. My ears pricked. A jingle in the night?

Breathing deeply, I picked up the scent of the slave catchers' horses. They were hiding in the forest, waiting. And Katie had no idea.

"We're ready, Star," Katie whispered as she came up beside me. "Eliza is mounted on Bell. I told her we'd take her to Miss Biddle's house. Teacher will know where Eliza's mother is. She'll know what to do."

My ears flicked. I knew what I had to do, too. The slave catchers were watching the farm. I had to lead them away from Katie, Eliza, and Bell.

Mother, take Katie and Eliza to Miss Biddle's, I called. Katie led me outside and over to the mounting stump. When she flipped the reins over my head, I butted her hard in the chest, sending her flying.

Without a backward glance, I took off into the dark night, galloping straight for the forest, the slave catchers' horses, and danger.

8

A Race

I raced toward the slave catchers' hiding place. My plan was for them to chase after me. I would lead them away from Miss Biddle's house.

There was only a sliver of moon, but still

I wondered if they would see that no one was on my back or if they would fall for my trick.

I galloped into the forest, spying the two horses hidden in a thicket. With a cry of "After them!" the slave catchers took off. I heard their whips crack against their horses' sides. I heard the clank of their spurs.

Stretching out my neck, I flew through the forest. My eyes quickly grew used to the dark. My hooves dug sure-footedly into the rocky earth. My sturdy legs leaped over logs and rocks.

The slave catchers' horses might have been fast Thoroughbreds, but they weren't Morgans, bred for the rocky Vermont countryside. They didn't know the paths made by

the deer or the lanes that twined through the maple groves. And they didn't know I'd beaten Billy Barton and Prince.

As I ran, I forgot all about the day's plowing. The cool night air blew through my mane.

The loose reins slapped against my neck as I led the slave catchers higher and higher—far from the river and Miss Biddle's house.

Behind me, I heard blowing and snorting and the thudding of hooves as the slave catchers' horses tried to keep up. But then the thudding abruptly stopped.

Puzzled, I slowed. The slave catchers had pulled up. "That horse is leading us nowhere," the tall one said. "We need to search the farm."

They turned their horses, spurring them hard. If they went back to the farm and woke Papa, someone would discover that Katie was gone. I needed to warn my mistress and Eliza.

I set off down the mountain, cutting through the maple grove to town. I had trotted many times past Miss Biddle's house, which was on the way to school.

Taking the short way, I arrived at Miss Biddle's. I spotted Bell standing by the front porch.

She startled when I trotted up beside her. I was breathing heavily and my neck was slippery with sweat.

What happened? she asked. *We saw you run into the forest. We heard the men call, "After them!"*

I will explain later. Where are Katie and Eliza?

Inside with Miss Biddle. They are taking Eliza north in Miss Biddle's carriage.

They'll never get away in time! I whinnied shrilly, and Katie ran onto the porch.

"Star! You're safe!"

How could I tell her that Eliza was not safe? How could I tell her the slave catchers were coming?

Bell understood. Together we pawed the lawn. We tossed our heads. We pranced in the direction of *north* and the *river*.

"Eliza!" Katie shouted into the house. "We must leave, *now*."

Eliza and Miss Biddle ran onto the porch. "Child, what is it?" Miss Biddle asked.

"The slave catchers are after Eliza." Grabbing Eliza's hand, Katie ran down the steps. "We have to hurry." Katie tossed Eliza onto Bell's back. "Hold tightly to Bell's mane. We must ride fast."

I swung beside the steps so Katie could mount. She jumped onto my back. Bell and I cantered from Miss Biddle's house down to the river. I kept looking around, watching for the slave catchers.

By the time we reached the river, dawn was breaking. We trotted upstream along the bank to a crossing. Here the water was shallow, and the bottom was rocky enough for wagons to cross.

Katie's heels nudged me into the swirling water. It felt cool on my tired legs and sweaty

neck. The girls were silent as Bell and I sloshed across.

I kept my ears pricked, listening for sounds behind us and ahead of us. The sky was changing from black to gray. Lifting my nose, I sniffed. *Horses*.

Someone was riding along the bank we had just left. I broke into a trot and clambered from the water. Stopping, I stared across the river. I saw two men on horses silhouetted against the morning sky. It was the slave catchers.

9

North

"Star?" Katie whispered. "What is it?" Then she must have seen the slave catchers, too, because she gasped in fear.

Eliza cried out, "Don't let me be caught, miss!"

"Never." Katie slid off my back. "Star and

I promised to take you to freedom, didn't we?" Reaching up, she helped Eliza off Bell.

I heard the slave catchers shout. Had they seen us? Would there be time to get away?

Katie handed Eliza a bundle. "This lane leads north to Canada. Miss Biddle will get word to your mother to meet you."

The two girls hugged. "Thank you, Miss Katie," Eliza whispered. "You have been a true, brave friend."

Tears sprang into Katie's eyes. "*You* are the bravest girl, Eliza. But you'll need more than bravery to get you to Canada. You'll need Star."

Me? I'm going to Canada?

Then I heard a *splash* as the slave catchers' horses plunged into the river. Katie was right.

If Eliza didn't flee with me now, we would all meet danger. I glanced at Katie. Bell would make sure that Katie returned home safely. I had to make sure Eliza reached Canada safely.

Katie boosted Eliza onto my back. "Star will take care of you," she said. As she kissed me goodbye, tears streamed down her cheeks. "Take care of Star, Eliza," she whispered, and then, stepping back, she swatted me hard on the flank and yelled, "Run, Star!"

I bolted up the riverbank, Bell's whinny goodbye following after me, Katie's cry, "Run!" echoing in my ears.

Eliza clung to my mane as I raced up the lane, which soon turned into a steep, narrow trail. Sharp rocks hurt my hooves. Branches slapped my face.

But I couldn't stop. The slave catchers' horses were close behind.

Flattening my ears, I pretended I was racing Prince. I pretended I was flying wildly through the meadow. I pretended I was galloping to *wherever I wanted*.

My legs stretched long and high as I bounded over ledges and streams and through the thick forest. How long did I gallop? How long did Eliza clutch my mane with all her might? How long before the slave catchers' horses fell behind?

I do not know. But suddenly the only hoofbeats I heard were my own.

Stopping behind an outcropping of rock, I peered down the rough trail. My sides heaved.

My breath roared in my nostrils. Eliza panted just as loudly as I.

"We lost them," she whispered. Slowly, her fingers loosened in my mane.

I listened. Except for us, the woods were indeed quiet.

"We lost them!" Dropping onto my neck, Eliza hugged me. "Thank you, Star. You are as

wonderful as your mistress. Now all we need to do is find Canada and my mama."

Turning north, I again headed up the mountain. My hooves were chipped. My legs were tired. The forest grew thicker. The morning sun rose higher, bringing the heat and the flies. Eliza slapped, and I swatted. When I thought I couldn't take another step, the trees opened into a small clearing.

I stopped in my tracks. A cluster of cabins stood in the clearing. Smoke rose from several chimneys. A milk cow chewed hay in front of a shed. Goats bleated in a small pen. Chickens scratched in the leaves. A small plot of ground had been cleared for planting. It looked much like home.

I heard the sound of an ax blade on wood. I heard human voices.

Is this north? I wondered. *Is this Canada and freedom? Is this where Eliza will be safe?*

Eliza sat still and watchful on my back. Then a woman came running from one of the cabins. She held her arms wide. "Eliza!" she called over and over as she ran toward us, her bare feet catching in her long skirts. Then a man hurried from behind a tree, an ax in his hand.

"Mama! Papa!" Eliza slid off my back. She hobbled toward her mother, falling into her arms.

Her father rushed over. "Thank heaven you're safe," he exclaimed as he, too, hugged Eliza.

"The teacher sent word you were coming," the father said. "We hunted for you this
morning when it turned light but found no
trace of you. How did you ever make it here
by yourself?"

"I wasn't by myself." Pulling away from
them, Eliza limped back to me. "Star was with
me. He brought me all the way from Vermont."

"Thank you, Star." I felt their grateful pats. Eliza's father led me to the shed. I drank deeply from a water bucket. Eliza took off my bridle and helped rub me with a feed sack until I was dry and cool. Then they fed me some of their milk cow's hay, and I ate hungrily.

When I was finally full, I lifted my head. Eliza, her mother, and her father were sitting on the porch of their cabin. Their arms were around each other as they talked excitedly.

I looked around, realizing that I *had* found north and freedom. Yet this place called Canada was much like the farm where I lived. Except there was no fence to hold me in.

Eliza and her mama were no longer slaves. They were free. I was free, too. Free to go to the place called *wherever I wanted.*

I pictured the tears rolling down Katie's cheeks when I galloped away. And suddenly I knew exactly where that place was.

Tired no longer, I trotted from the shed, across the clearing and into the forest. I found the path, and breaking into a canter, I headed toward Vermont, home, my mother, and Katie.

APPENDIX

MORE ABOUT THE
MORGAN HORSE

The First Morgan Horse

A small bay stallion named Figure is considered the first Morgan horse. Figure was foaled in Massachusetts in 1789. His sire (father) is believed to have been True Briton. When Figure was a few years old, he was traded to Justin Morgan. Morgan was a teacher and musician. He was also a horse breeder and bred Figure's dam (mother). In 1788, Morgan moved his family from Massachusetts, settling in Vermont.

Figure had an arched neck that made him look proud; a sleek, soft coat; a gentle disposition; and unusual strength for his size. Morgan rented out his horse for pulling stumps and logs. In 1795, Justin Morgan traded Figure for land. In 1796, Figure raced against the New York horses Sweepstakes and Silvertail. He defeated both, and the road where they raced is still called Morgan Mile. Figure's abilities made him a popular sire in New England. He passed on his fine qualities to his many children. All Morgan horses are related to Figure.

In 1798, Justin Morgan died. Folks began calling Figure "Justin Morgan" after his first owner. By this time, Figure had been traded or sold to several different owners. In 1817, Figure paraded through the town of Montpelier, Vermont. His rider was President James Monroe. Figure died at thirty-two years old, after he was kicked by another horse.

Morgans in History

In the 1850s, when Star tells his story, Morgan horses continued to be in demand. Folks loved them for their speed, personality, beauty, endurance, and strength. Green Mountain Morgan was a popular stallion who resembled Figure. Black Hawk, another Morgan stallion, was famous for his speed and showy gaits. New Englanders continued to want Morgan horses for daily chores. But they also sold Morgan horses to people in big cities like New York, where they were used for pulling carriages, stagecoaches, and freight wagons. They were also raced. When the West was settled, they were used as ranch horses. During the Civil War, about a thousand Morgan horses were used as cavalry mounts. The First Vermont Cavalry rode only Morgans.

The Morgan is considered America's oldest breed. In 1909, the Morgan Horse Club was formed. It started at a fair in Vermont where Morgan owners met to show off their horses. In 1971, the name was changed to the American Morgan Horse Association. Purebred Morgans are registered with the AMHA. The association keeps records of Morgans in the United States and other countries.

Morgans Today

Like Figure, today's Morgan horses have an upright neck; a muscular body; smooth, stylish gaits; a gentle personality; a thick mane and tail; and a sleek coat. They are known for their wide foreheads, large eyes, and small ears. Most range in size from fourteen and a half hands to fifteen and a half hands. (A

hand is four inches. A horse is measured from the ground to its withers.)

Morgan horses continue to be popular all-around horses. Families ride them on trails and in their backyards. Riders show them in Western and English classes and in endurance races and parades. They are also harnessed and driven in carriage competitions and for fun. Morgans make excellent horses for mounted police, but unlike Figure and Star, most are used for pleasure, not work.

About 107,950 living Morgan horses are registered with the American Morgan Horse Association. For a horse to be eligible, both parents must be Morgans.

Life in the 1850s

Life in Vermont was hard. Summer was short, winter was long, and spring brought the muddy season. Like Katie's family, most Vermonters lived on small farms. To survive, they grew crops, tended orchards, raised sheep, hunted, fished, and made maple syrup. In the 1840s, the price of wool had fallen, and many sheep farmers moved west to cheaper land. Many Vermont farmers switched to dairy cows. In 1848, Vermont's first railroad carried milk, cheese, and butter into New York and Boston. Still, many farmers, both men and women, left the land to work in factories in Vermont and Massachusetts.

Vermont and Slavery

Vermont was the first state to free its slaves after the Revolutionary War. By 1837, the state had eighty-nine antislavery groups. Folks in Vermont were active in the Underground Railroad, a network of safe houses to help slaves escaping to Canada. By 1833, Canada had outlawed slavery and did not allow slave catchers into the country.

In 1850, the Fugitive Slave Law was enacted by the United States government. This law stated that no citizen in any state could help runaway slaves. People who protected runaways risked punishment. Slave hunters and bounty hunters roamed Vermont and other Northern states searching for runaways.

Despite the law, whites and free blacks continued to help slaves find their way to Canada. Vermont borders Canada, so the state was one route to freedom. St. Albans, Vermont, is about thirteen miles from the border.

Many runaway slaves like Eliza and her parents settled in Canada. They worked hard to build homes and outbuildings, clear ground for farming, and obtain cows, pigs, and horses. By 1850, the town of Dawn, Ontario, home to five hundred black settlers, had a sawmill, a rope factory, and a brick-yard.

Turn the page for a special preview
of the next Horse Diaries book.

Independence, Missouri,
Early Spring, 1846

On that quiet spring morning, there was nothing but green grass and sun and the smell of my mama. I nuzzled her and she moved closer, so I could have more of her warm, sweet milk. There was so much I didn't know yet, so much that she promised to show me. But I had already found out scores of things on my own. I was just three days old, but I bet I knew more than lots of older horses. I knew that the small white fur-balls on the hillside that Mama called sheep didn't care at all about playing. They didn't care even if I pranced up to them and said, *Come on, let's play.* And they sure didn't want to race. There were other things on that hillside that looked kind of like sheep. But they didn't move at all, and that's how I learned they were rocks.

Rocks just sit in one place all day long, year after year, my mama said, *just soaking up sun and snow, which comes later.*

But rocks didn't move at all, even when

I nudged one with my nose. I was awful glad that I wasn't born a rock.

My mama told me, and then told me again, that I was much too curious. She told me I had to watch out and not get too bold. But she was gentle when she said these things. I knew she liked my spirit, and I told her that I liked my spirit, too. My mama whinnied when I told her that. Then she told me to lie down and rest because we had a long day ahead. We were heading back to the herd, she said. She'd gone off alone for a time, away from the herd, once she knew that I was about to be born. She wanted me all to herself for a while, and I understood that. Like I told my mama, I was learning a whole lot of things already.

Still, why rest when the sun was up and shining, and the wind was blowing like anything? So just for fun, I went zooming around the hillside, my mane flying in the wind. I felt the sun, warm on my back. My legs had been all wobbly for the first day or so, but not now. Now, they felt like they were attached to me real good. They moved me along so fast I was even leaping around at times. And then I saw something new.

It was small, sort of round, with prickly things on it. And it wasn't moving. Well, how could anything not move on a day like this?

I nosed up to it.

No, it wasn't a rock. Then why hold so still? It had pointing kinds of things sticking out all over its body. It seemed to be looking at me. Even now, young as I was, I knew that rocks didn't look at you. I placed my nose down close.

And then, like the wind itself had roared up to my side, suddenly my mama was there. Her body seemed to swell, filling the air beside me. I could feel the heat of her nearness. Her eyes were wild, her ears laid back.

Foolish colt! she said. *Come away! Now.*

She shoved her shoulder into me, almost making me fall to the ground. I backed away.

Follow me. Come! she said.

And she turned tail, flying back up the hillside toward the trees where we had been. I liked this race, and I ran on ahead. But my mama caught up and passed me. She stopped short, so short that I couldn't stop. I bumped her big side. Then I tumbled back a bit. I stumbled over a rock, and then I was lying on the ground. I looked up at her, surprised. I got my long legs back under me and untangled myself and stood up. But one leg ached. When I looked down, I saw a thin stream of blood running down my flank.

Was this some kind of game? I didn't like it.

No, it wasn't a game. I had not seen my mama like this before, but I knew what it was. She was very angry.

She lowered her head and looked in my eyes. *That was a porcupine. It could prick those quills right into your face. They would hurt worse than that fall you just took.*

Oh.

My pride was wounded, so I looked away. *It doesn't hurt much*, I said.

Never mind hurt! my mama said, still angry-like. *Those quills get in your face and you would swell all up. You wouldn't be able to eat. To nurse. You'd starve to death.*

Well, I knew enough by now to know that I had just been born, and I sure liked it here. And I knew that death wouldn't be what I'd want for a real long time.

I hung my head, real ashamed-like. I guess I did have a lot to learn.

Curious is good, my mama said, and now she sounded not as angry. *Foolish is not!*

Yes, Mama.

She seemed to relent some because she whinnied at me, telling me to look up. I did, and looked high in the sky. There were birds flying all about, wild black ones, and one that soared and swooped low. Mama said the soaring one was an eagle. I wondered what it would be like to be born an eagle, to have wings instead of legs and hooves. Then we saw an ugly-faced one that kept swooping down to look at something on the hillside.

My mama got quiet when that big bird swooped by, and she didn't say anything about it, but I could tell that she didn't like it much. I nudged myself closer, and Mama nudged me back.

What, Mama? I asked her.

A *buzzard*, my mama answered. *They're mean old birds. Come only when something is dead or dying.*

And then, because my mama was a little quiet, and I knew I had frightened her with that porcupine, and maybe she was thinking that buzzard would come for me if I was dead, well, I decided maybe she needed me to rest right close by her side for a while.

I closed my eyes and lay down, my legs stretched out. The sun was warm, and so many things whirled around inside my head. My mama was nearby. She liked my spirit. And soon we would go back and meet the herd. Mama said most of the herd horses were like us, quarter horses. That meant we could run very, very fast, the fastest quarter mile that any horse on earth could run. Well, I knew that. I knew I was the fastest horse already. I flicked my ears a little bit when I slept, just to let Mama know I was still there with her, maybe dreaming some. And then she was nudging me.

Time to get up, my little colt.

Well, she didn't have to tell me twice.

I was up and ready to go, wanting so much to go back to those other horses Mama had told me about. She told me then what the others would call me. I had been given a name already. Koda, it was. She said that it had a special meaning, but she wouldn't tell me what it was. She said I would find out, but not yet.

About the Author

Alison Hart has been horse-crazy ever since she can remember. A teacher and author, she has written more than twenty books for children, most of them about horses. She loves to write about the past, when horses like Bell's Star were valuable in everyday life. Her novel *Shadow Horse* was nominated for an Edgar Award. Today Ms. Hart still rides, because—you guessed it— she's still horse-crazy!

About the Illustrator

Ruth Sanderson grew up with a love for horses. She drew them constantly, and her first oil painting at age fourteen was a horse portrait.

Ruth has illustrated and retold many fairy tales and likes to feature horses in them whenever possible. Her book about a magical horse, *The Golden Mare, the Firebird, and the Magic Ring*, won the Texas Bluebonnet Award in 2003. She illustrated the first Black Stallion paperback covers and has illustrated a number of chapter book horse stories, most recently *Summer Pony* and *Winter Pony* by Jean Slaughter Doty.

Ruth and her daughter have two horses, an Appaloosa named Thor and a quarter horse named Gabriel. She lives with her family in Massachusetts.

To find out more about her adventures with horses and the research she did to create the illustrations in this book, visit her Web site, www.ruthsanderson.com.

Collect all the books in the
Horse Diaries series!

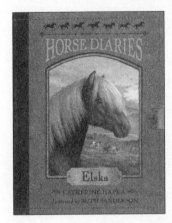

And coming soon

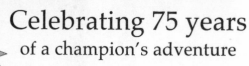